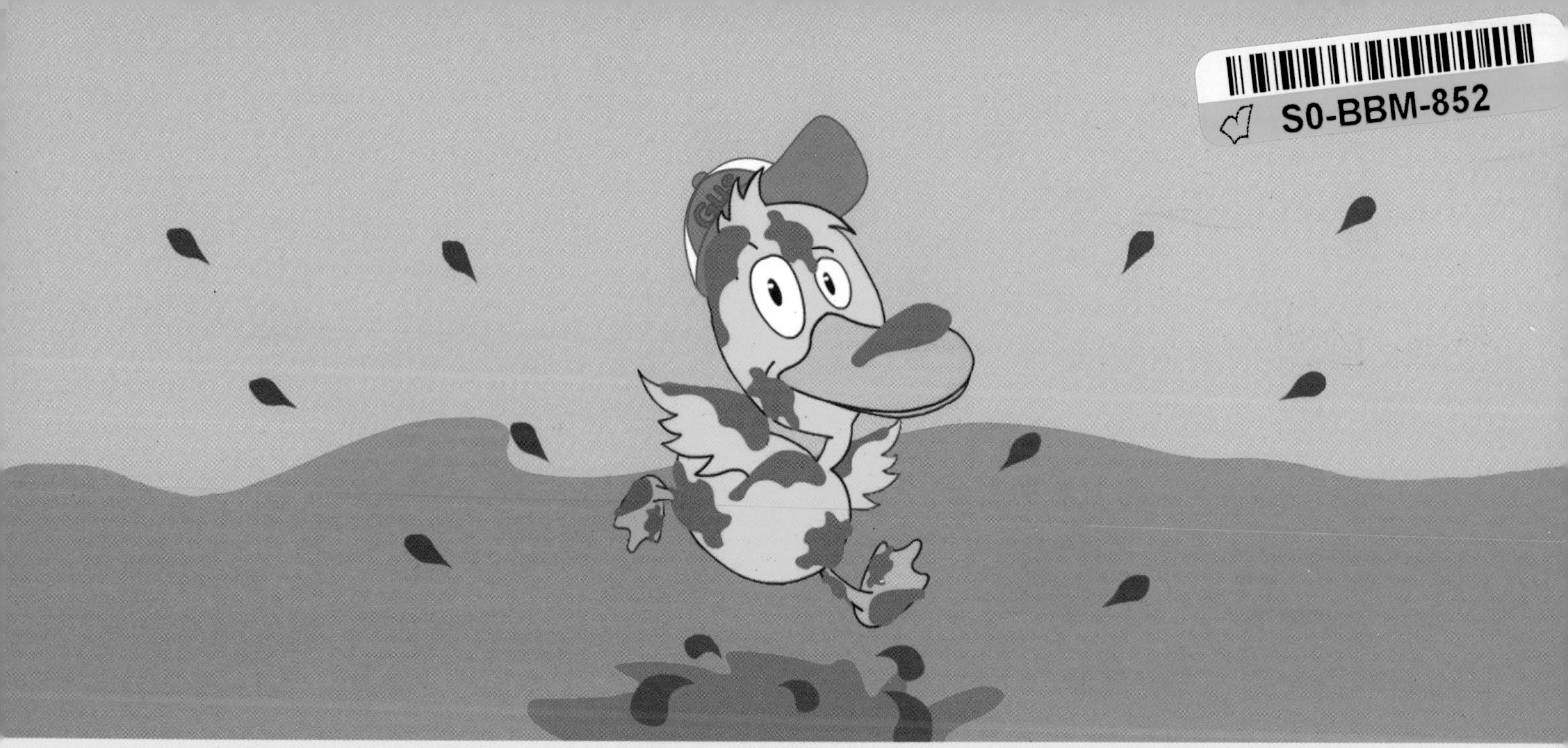

Gus runs in the mud.

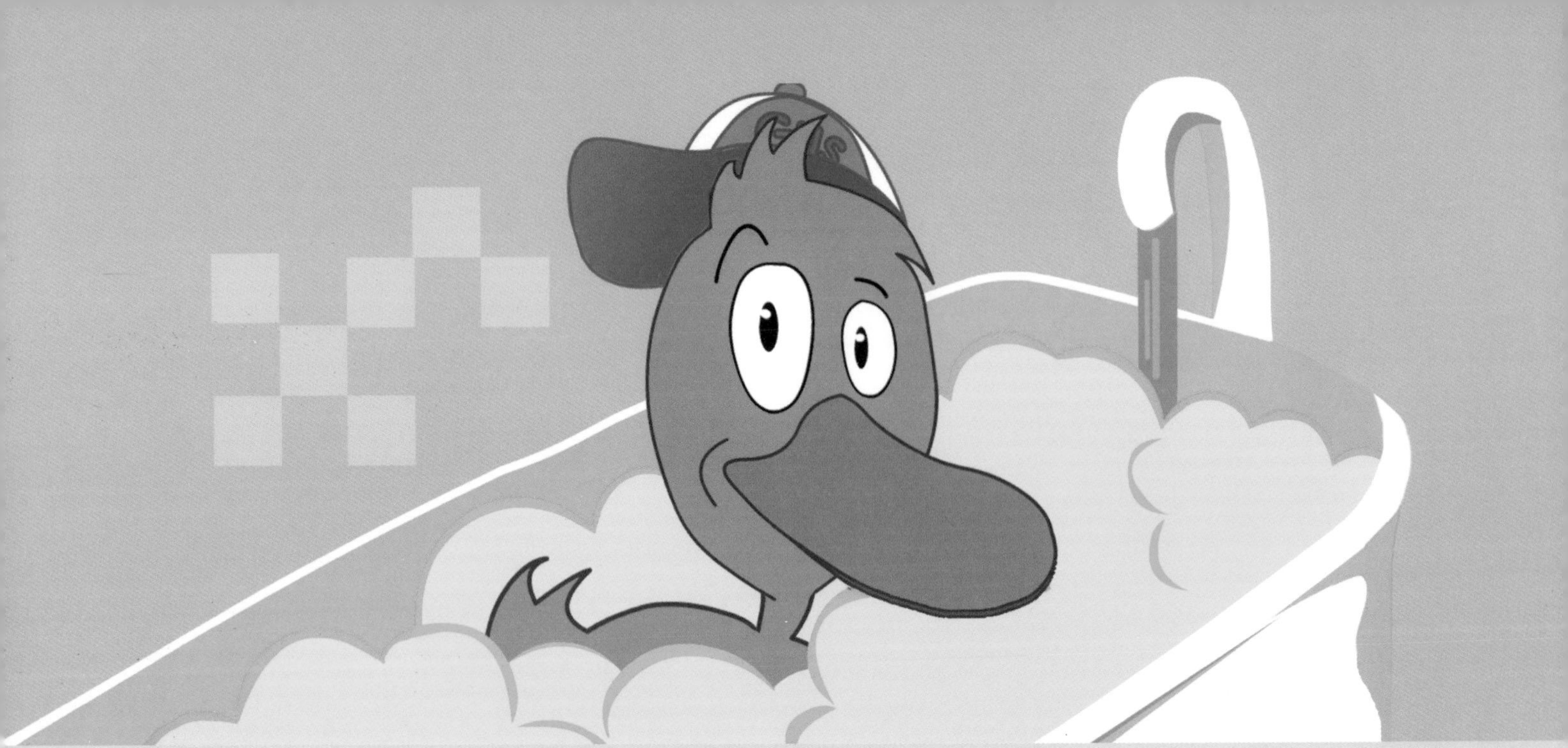

Gus gets in the tub.

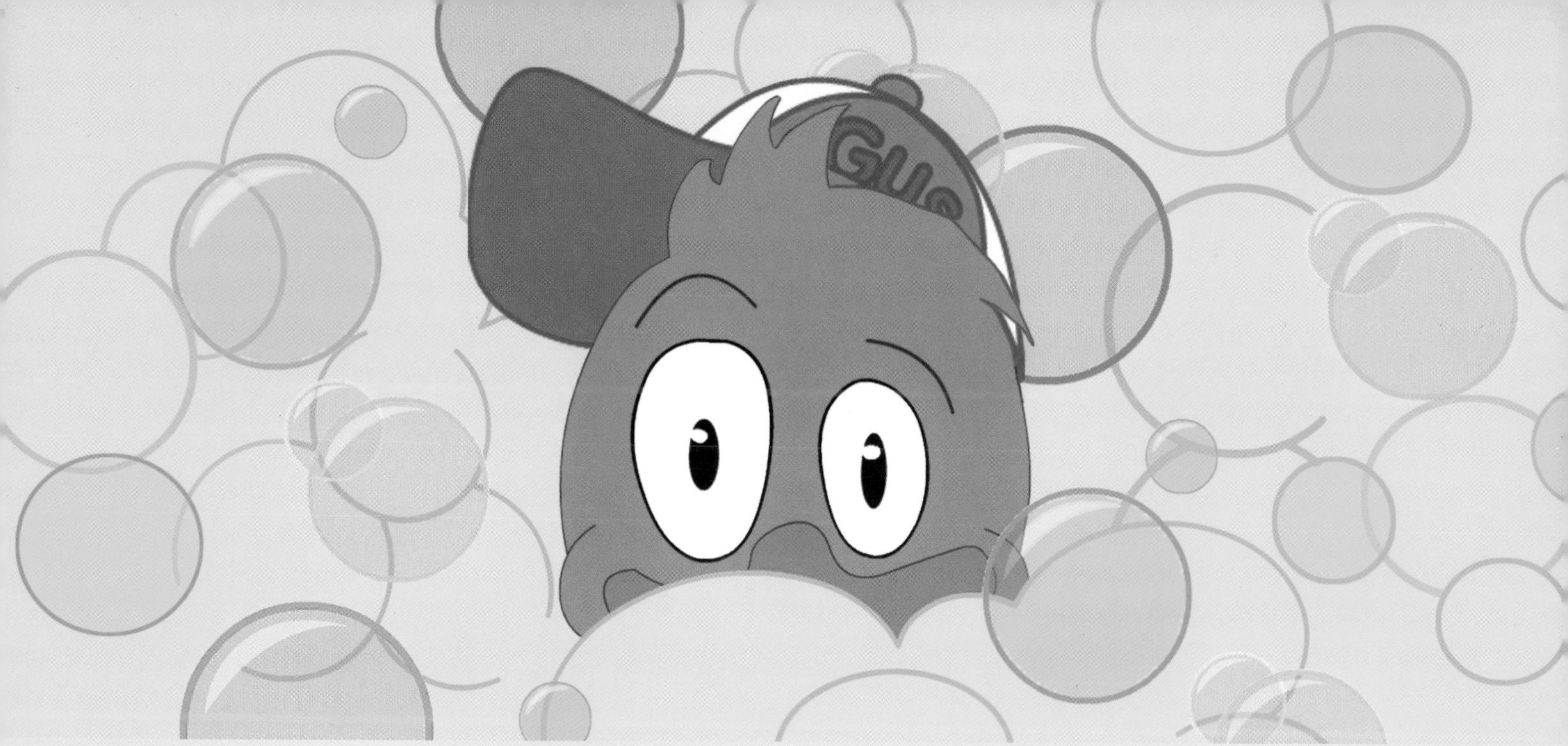

The tub has suds.

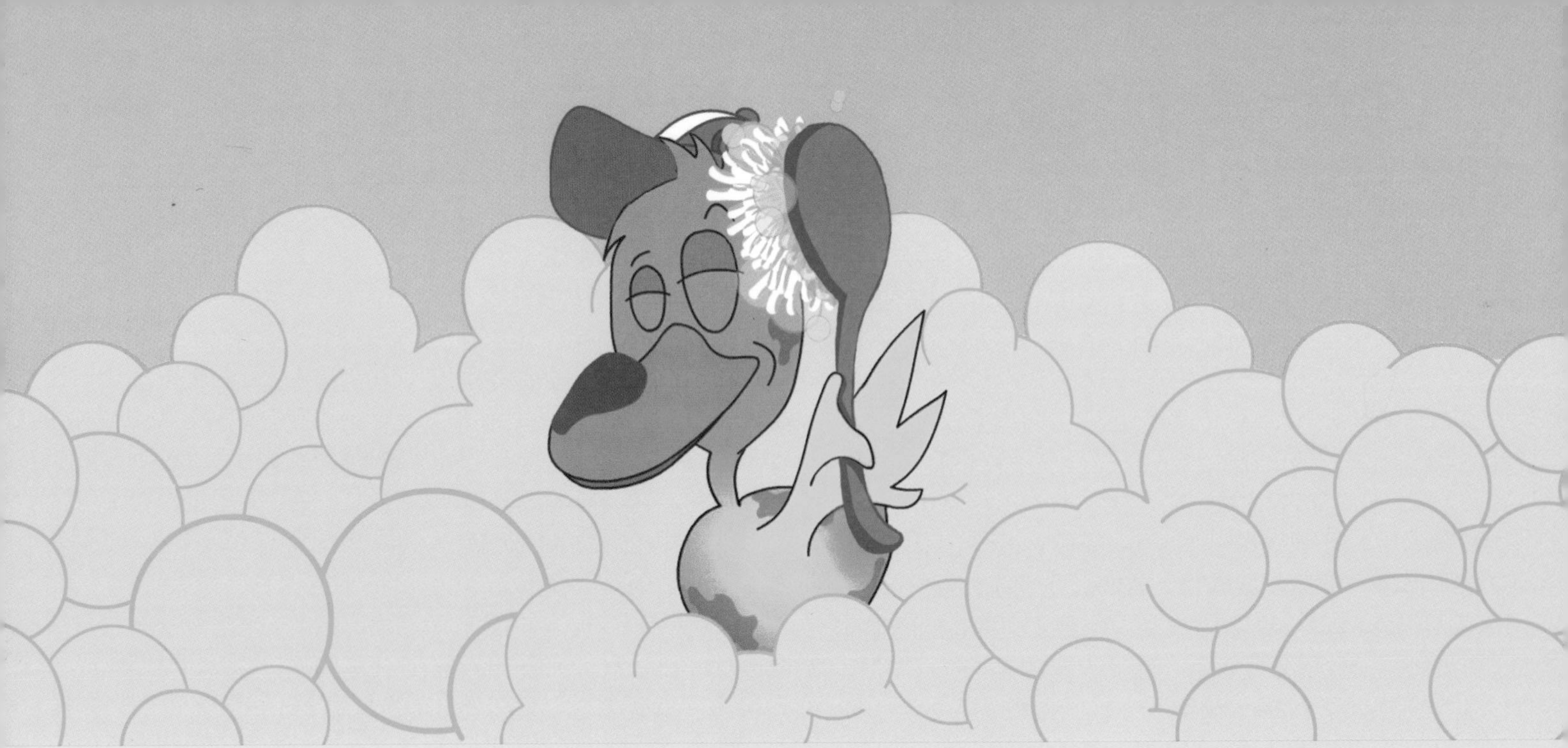

Gus rubs and rubs.

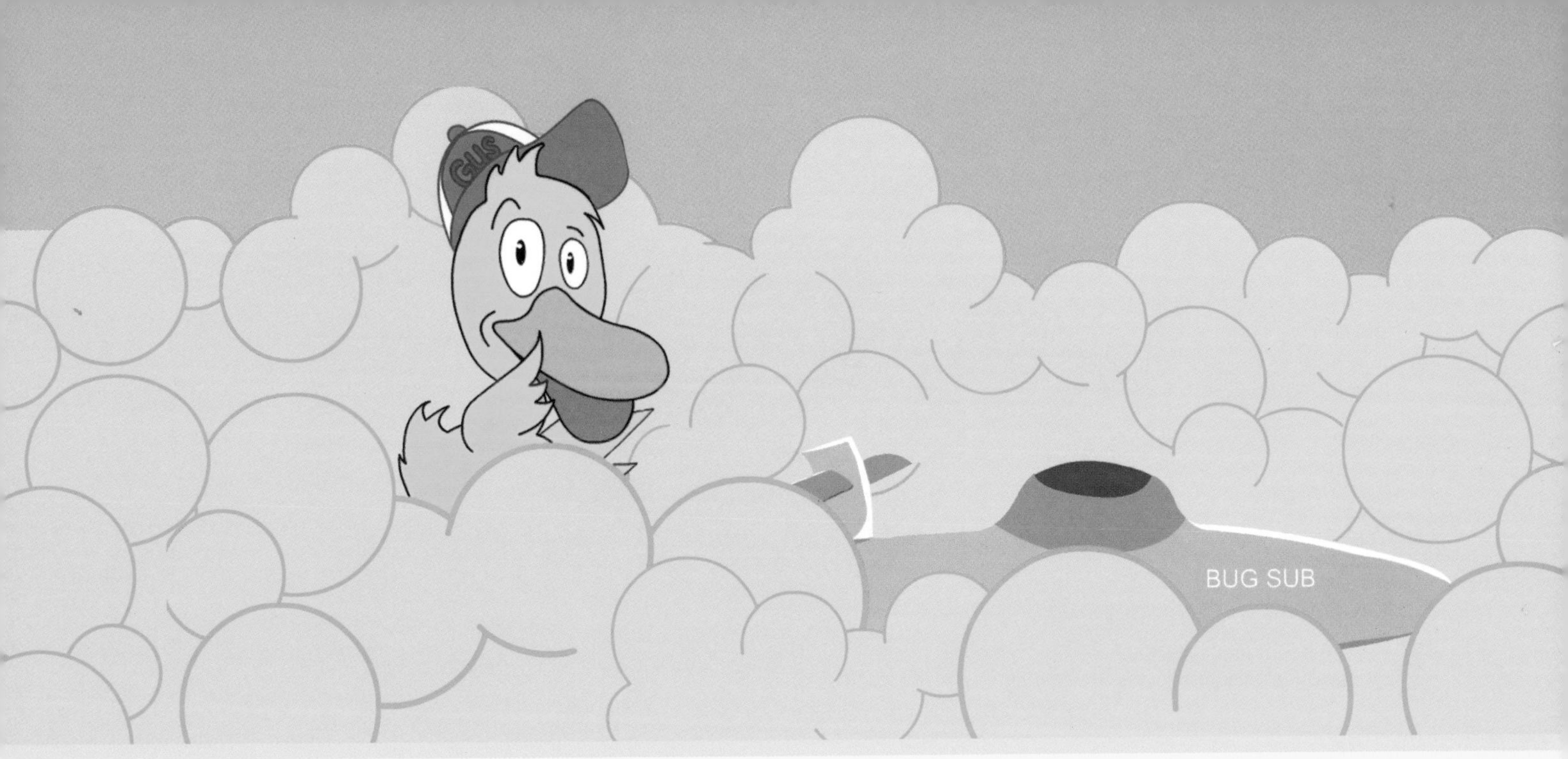

Gus has a sub.

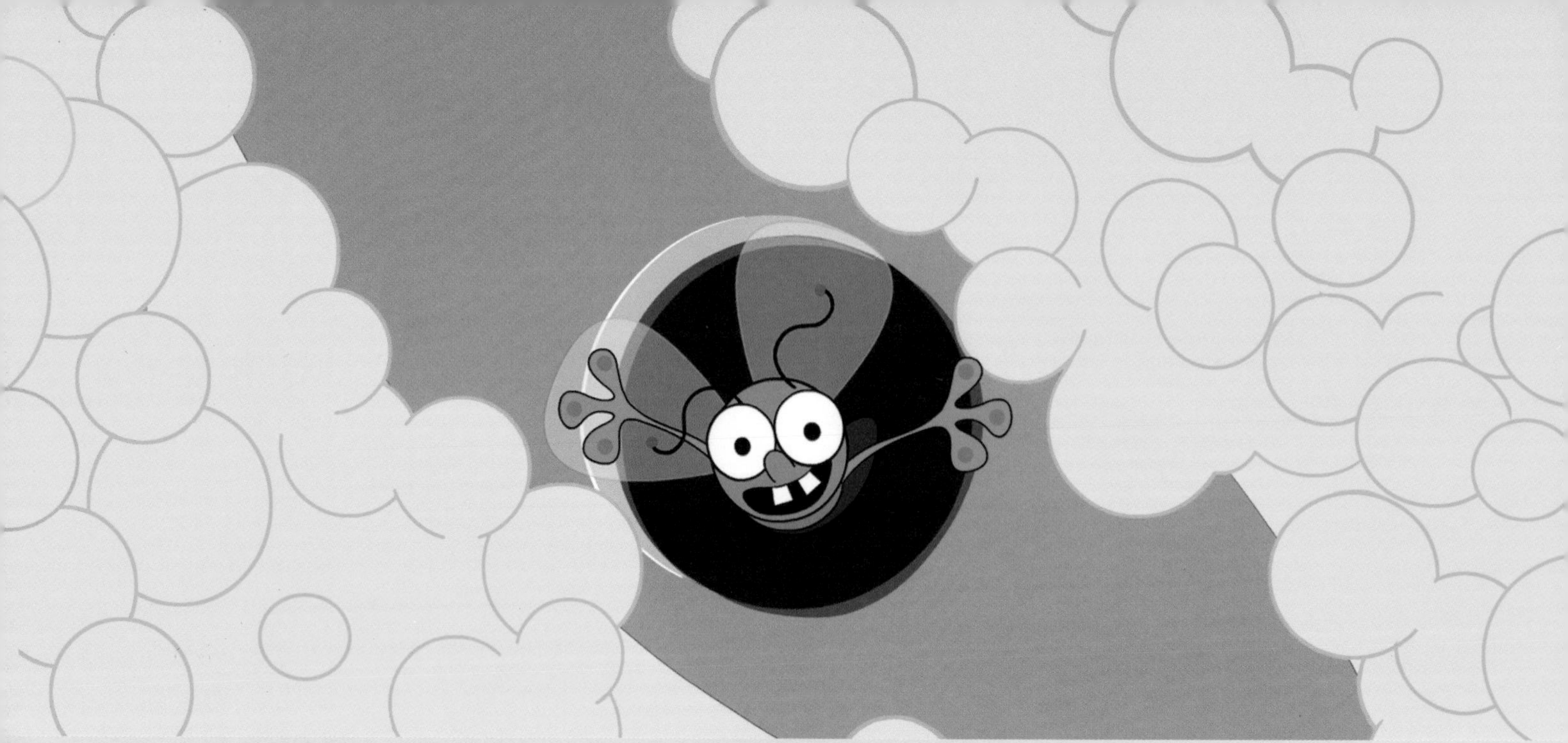

A bug is in the sub!

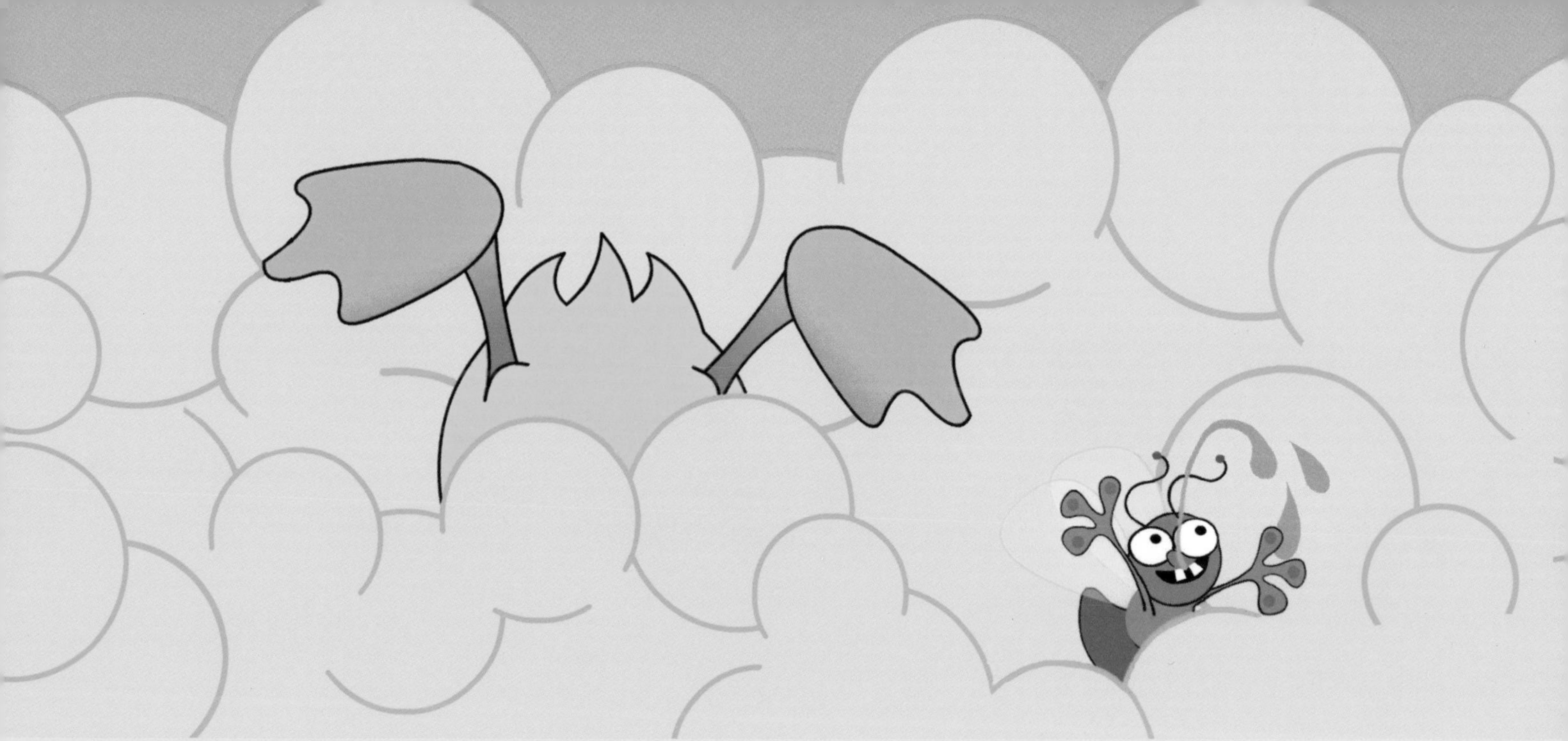

It is fun in the tub.

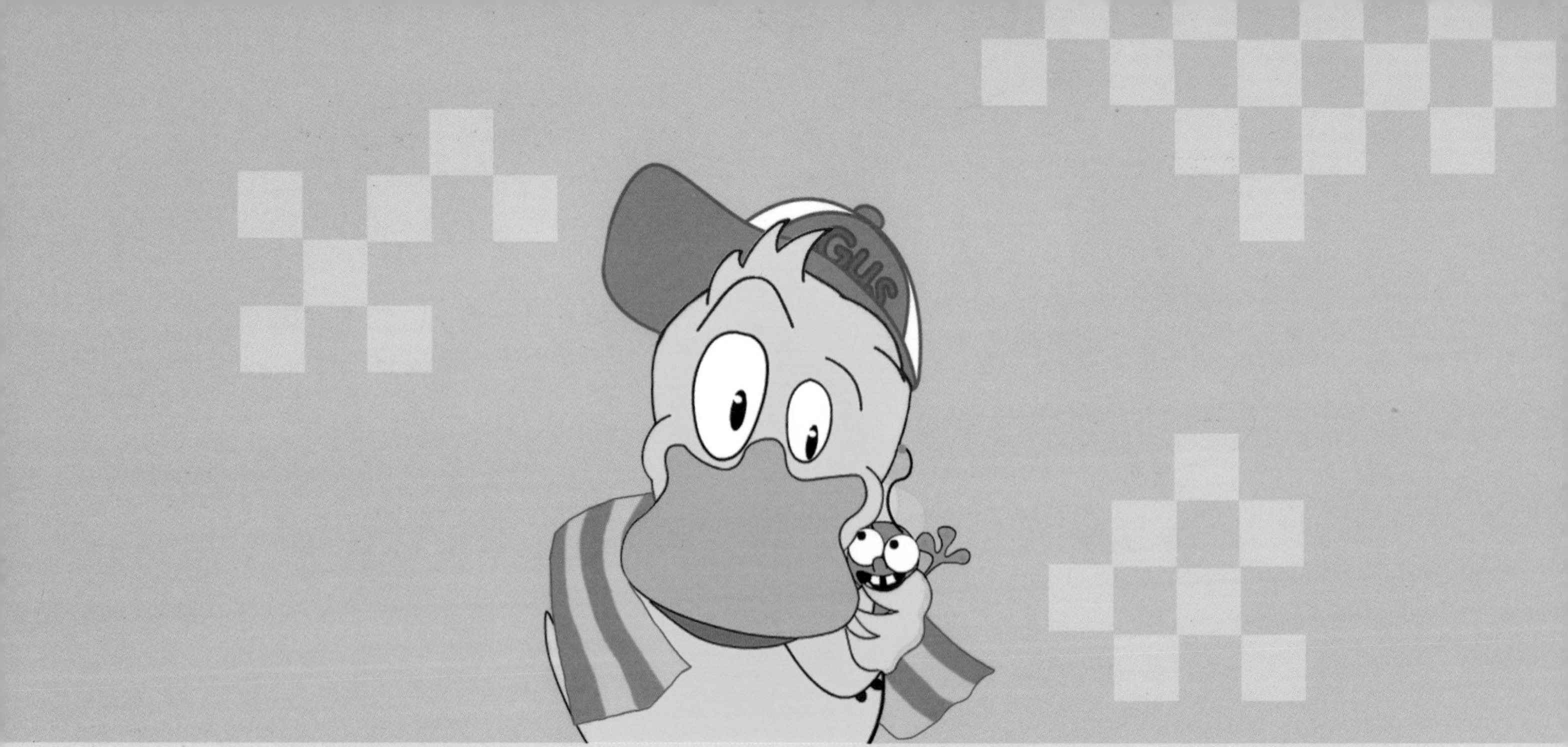

Gus hugs the bug.

The end